There was something on my head, all right. I could feel it. . . .

A small, pointed feathered head peeked down. Beady bird eyes blinked.

"Get off my head!"

"Okay—if you'll eat me."

"No."

The beady bird eyes blinked again. The corners of the beak wiggled down to a frown.

"What do you mean, no?"

"No means *no!* I don't eat birds."

"What do you mean, you don't eat birds?"

"Well, when I was little I was attacked by a mad rooster . . . ."

"Look, Cat," the bird interrupted, "I don't want your life history. I just want to get it over with. . . ."

"Look, bird, I wish I could help you, but—"

"Just my luck," she chirped. "I'm starving to death and I land on the only cat in the country who won't eat birds. If you won't eat me, then feed me!"

Books by Carol and Bill Wallace

The Flying Flea, Callie, and Me

Available from MINSTREL Books

Books by Bill Wallace

Red Dog
Trapped in Death Cave

Available from ARCHWAY Paperbacks

The Backward Bird Dog
Beauty
The Biggest Klutz in Fifth Grade
Blackwater Swamp
Buffalo Gal
The Christmas Spurs
Danger in Quicksand Swamp
Danger on Panther Peak
  (*Original title:* Shadow on the Snow)
A Dog Called Kitty
Eye of the Great Bear
Ferret in the Bedroom, Lizards in the Fridge
The Final Freedom
Journey into Terror
Never Say Quit
Snot Stew
Totally Disgusting!
True Friends
Upchuck and the Rotten Willy
Upchuck and the Rotten Willy: The Great Escape
Watchdog and the Coyotes

Available from MINSTREL Books

Carol Wallace and Bill Wallace

The Flying Flea, Callie, and Me

ILLUSTRATED BY DAVID SLONIM

A
MINSTREL®
BOOK

Published by POCKET BOOKS
New York   London   Toronto   Sydney   Tokyo   Singapore

A Minstrel Book published by
POCKET BOOKS, a division of Simon & Schuster Inc.
1230 Avenue of the Americas, New York, NY 10020

ISBN: 0-671-03968-7

First Minstrel Books printing September 1999

10 9 8 7 6 5 4 3 2 1

To my second grade class of 1996–97: Jamie Burnes, Chip Collins, Tracy Couch, Amanda Curtis, Rollo Dickenson, Nathan Gorham, Erica Heath, Jessica Hill, Mimi Huber, Damon Logue, Keith Mangus, Michelle Rose, Douglas Sanders, Cassie Stanley, Ben Still, Emily Summars, Tiara Thomas, and Christopher Wentz

CHAPTER 1

I strolled toward the porch with my trophy. My feet and tail were wet from the morning dew. The night hunt had been a good one. I climbed the steps and dropped the remains of the last mouse on the mat. The House Mama would be *so proud* of me when she found it. From the porch I could see the hayfield where the mice played every night. Most of them were sleeping now, but when it got dark I would return for another hunt.

The leaves of the apple tree near the driveway shook from the gentle summer breeze as I walked down the sidewalk away from the house.

My whiskers twitched when I saw Mockingbird fly back and forth from the pasture to the apple tree. I sat down to wash my front paws.

She seemed to be working very hard adding twigs to the pile she was collecting on a branch.

I trotted toward the woodpile under the apple tree. As soon as Bird flew off to the pasture once more, I hopped up the stacked logs to take a look for myself. A soft hissing sound came from beneath the woodpile. I stopped, frowning at the strange noise. Suddenly Bird swooped down at me. I flattened myself as close to the woodpile as I could. My ears pressed down against my head. With every muscle tensed, I waited for her next attack. Sure enough, she hit me. I flinched. It was only a warning peck on the side of my face.

Bird flew at me again, fast and accurate. This time she pecked me on the top of my head. I swished my tail as I stretched my claws, trying to hold on to the woodpile. She started on another fly-by. The wind from her wings made my hair rustle.

"Leave my nest alone, Gray Cat!" Bird screamed.

I really wanted to see what she was doing with the messy pile of twigs. Instead I hopped to the ground and fluffed my fur. My tail flipped back and forth when I walked to the holly bushes in front of the house. I needed a quick nap before going back to the tree. Bird watched me as I nestled behind a bush. I was safe here from her attacks.

I had been on the farm for just a short time. The House People had picked me out of my litter to be a mouser. My mother was the best mouser ever. She had taught me how to sneak up, without making so much as a sound. She had taught me how to crouch. Best of all she had taught me how to pounce. She could catch a mouse every time she went hunting—well, almost every time. I wasn't quite that good yet, but I got better every day.

The House People had said that Callie was getting too old to keep up with the mouse problem. Most of her days she spent sleeping in the sun. At night she slept inside on a bed.

Bird's shrill call woke me. My whiskers sprang up. I opened one eye and watched her swoop. She pecked Callie as the old cat walked from the field to the house I stretched both front legs and stood up.

"Hey, leave Callie alone. She's old. She isn't bothering you!"

"Mind your own business, Gray Cat! I have my work to do, and Callie knows it!"

I quickly trotted out to meet Callie. When Bird

swooped again, I swiped at her with my sharp claws.

"You missed me, Cat!" she scoffed as she flew up to the apple tree.

Callie strolled to the porch and jumped onto the rocking chair. "Thanks for the help. Bird has been working hard on her nest in the apple tree. She will be laying her eggs soon. That should keep her busy for a while so we can get some rest."

Laying eggs? Nest? After a short catnap I just *had* to see what Bird was doing with the twigs. The grass felt dry on my paws now. I crept around the long way, through the pine trees, so Bird wouldn't see me. If I took a quick peek, I could be back on the porch before she ever spotted me.

As I neared the woodpile, I noticed something brown. It looked like the garden hose that the Mama used to water her flowers. A gentle rustling sound came to my ears when it moved. My head tilted to the side, and my whiskers sprang up. *The garden hose doesn't move,* I thought with a frown. I leaned forward for a closer look when the brown hose stopped, turned, and glared at me. When I blinked and took a step back, the hose slid toward the woodpile. Crouching close to the ground, I inched toward the end of the thing. I slapped at the pointed tip as it disappeared between two of the logs.

The hose hissed at me, really loud. I jumped back.

"Leave me alone!" the hiss said.

I couldn't see anything, but I knew a hose couldn't talk. Again I leaned closer. Bird swooped down at me. I backed up, then scampered for the pine trees.

"Cat, leave my nest alone!" Bird screamed again.

"I didn't do anything. I was looking at the hose under the woodpile!"

"Stay away!" Bird warned.

For three days Bird worked on the nest. She made trips to the field, then back to her tree. Callie and I were easy targets for her if we happened to cross her path. Callie didn't even flinch when Bird hit her. I tried to scare Bird with my claws. Sometimes I spun around, pretending to bite at her.

On the fourth day things were different. Callie noticed it first. "Bird hasn't been after us today."

"Where do you think she is?" I asked.

"She's probably laying her eggs." Callie stretched and yawned. "She usually has four or five eggs in her nest."

"How do you know?" I twitched my whiskers.

"The Mama Mockingbird has been coming back to that old tree for years. She thinks it is the best home for her family." Callie closed both eyes and curled up into a ball.

"Have you seen the eggs?"

"A few times," she answered without opening her eyes. "When I was younger, I would try to check out her eggs every year. Now it is too dangerous for me to climb very high. The people put the woodpile under the tree last year. It is a little easier to get to the nest now, but I would rather eat the nice soft cat food that I can get inside. There is no reason to risk getting caught up in the tree for those little birds. Besides, I like Bird. She is just doing her job, protecting her family. The Papa Mockingbird is around somewhere. He pecks, too. He watches from the pines."

Callie slept for a while. I listened for the Papa Mockingbird. The warm sunshine felt good on my coat. I took a long bath, washing with my tongue and paws. I would check that nest when Bird finished laying her eggs.

I was almost asleep when a sound in the grass made my ears perk up. Listening, I held my breath and tilted my head to one side. I saw the brown hose moving slowly across the yard. My ears were up, my legs ready to pounce. What was that strange hose that could move by itself?

I crouched, my tail twitching nervously. The brown hose slithered across the driveway and into the dirt. I followed it, one step at a time. The green garden hose that the Mama used to water her flowers didn't move by itself. Something deep inside told me to be careful.

As I eased closer, the brown hose disappeared back under the woodpile. Just then another bird dropped down and pecked me on the back near my tail. This wasn't a fly-by—this was a peck! It hurt, too. It also caught me by surprise. I had been concentrating so hard on the brown hose that I forgot all about the birds.

When the peck came, my front end stopped and backed up—only my back end jumped. It jumped really high, too. First thing I knew, my tail went over the top of my head. I saw it, but there was nothing I could do. My tail went, then my rear end. I was flat on my back.

We cats don't like to land on our backs. We are supposed to land on all fours. Quick as the blink of an eye, I twisted and scrambled to my feet. My tail flipped as I glanced around, hoping no one had seen me.

"Cat, get away from my family!" Papa Mockingbird sharpened his beak on the branch where he was perched. He glared at me with his black eyes.

CHAPTER 2

I flopped down on the porch. Licking my paw, I rubbed at the back of my neck where Papa Mockingbird had pecked me. It still hurt.

"Gray, you need to watch what you're doing when you go to the woodpile." Callie looked down at me from the rocker.

"I *was* watching. That bird pecked me for no reason. I was minding my own business!"

"No, I'm not talking about Bird. I mean Bullsnake," Callie purred.

"What's a bullsnake?"

"I saw you following Bullsnake across the yard. He is long and brown. You were creeping up on him." Callie jumped down from the rocker and stood in front of me. When she looked me straight in the eye, I blinked.

"Oh, the brown hose? What is it called?"

"His name is Bullsnake. He has lived around the barn for a long time. He helps me get rid of mice. Last year when the rats moved into the barn, he moved out. The rats were too big and scary, so now he lives under the woodpile."

I glanced toward the stacked logs. "Is he mean or nice?" I asked.

Callie shrugged her ears. "He's just Bullsnake. He leaves me alone, and I leave him alone."

The old cat walked to the corner and rolled in the dust. Then she curled up to take a nap. I decided to check out the hayfield. A few mice were out. I missed one but caught a small trophy to take home. As I crossed the front yard, Bird tapped me on the head. This time I was sort of expecting it. I still jumped, but I didn't flip myself over. Instead, I hurried to the house and dropped the mouse on the mat.

I spent most of my rest time on the porch. The house faced the place where the sun went to hide at night. Sometimes I would watch it slowly slide behind the rock hill across the road. In front of the rock hill was the hay field where the mice ate the farmer's crop. Closer to the house were pine trees. They were thick and bushy. There was a driveway between them and the apple tree. It was covered with little bitsy gray rocks. When the human people came home, they drove up the driveway and left their car under what they called a carport. It was like a house—with a roof but no walls. Around the corner from the carport was a chain-link fence. There was just enough room between the fence and the house so I could squeeze through and lie in the flowers in Mama's backyard. I had to watch for the dog, though. Her name was Muffy. She never chased me, because she was old, even older than Callie. Fact is, she hardly ever got up and moved around very much at all. Still, she was a dog, and cats just can't trust dogs.

I stayed on the porch resting and watching for long time. When Bird didn't fly from her nest, I walked to the woodpile. My tail gave a nervous flip. I took a deep breath and jumped up on the logs. Quiet as could be I climbed up to the first limb. A warning call came from inside the nest. Bird peeked over the pile of twigs.

"Don't even think about it, Cat! Get away! I have work to do. I don't have time to chase you right now." She fluffed her feathers.

A sudden sharp peck hit my head. The sneak attack startled me. I almost lost my hold on the tree bark.

"Stay out of our tree!" Papa Mockingbird scolded.

As I backed down from the limb, I stopped to

sharpen my claws on the bark. *That will show them I'm not scared*, I thought. *I need a nap anyway.*

I would wait until Papa Mockingbird went to the field to hunt. Then I would check the nest again. As I started to move away from the woodpile, I heard the strange hissing sound. I tried to peek inside but couldn't see anything. I backed up and pressed my body to the ground. I lay there for a long time.

"Bullsnake, is that you?"

"Leave me alone!" he hissed from inside the darkness.

"I'm new here and we haven't met. Don't you want to come out?"

"Leave me alone!" he hissed again.

I stared hard. My eyes narrowed to slits as I tried to see into the spaces between the logs. I finally stood up and sharpened my claws on Bull-snake's home—he needed to know I wasn't afraid of him, either. I strolled back to the edge of the driveway. Bird peeked over the edge of her nest and watched me walk back to the porch.

Callie had gone into the house when I returned. Papa Mockingbird sat near the top of the apple tree. He chirped and jabbered, but he never took his eyes off me. The trophy was missing from the mat. The House Mama must have found it. With a proud smile, I jumped onto the rocker.

I dreamed of juicy mice hiding in the field and the House Mama petting me and telling me what a great mouser I was.

A few days later I heard new sounds coming from the nest. I waited patiently under the holly bushes. When Bird flew to the field, I bounced up from my hiding place and took off for the tree. Papa Mockingbird pecked me on the back.

"Get away!" he warned.

Suddenly Bird was back on her nest. "Gray Cat, my babies aren't even big enough for a snack for you! Don't come here again!"

Papa Mockingbird's sharp beak stabbed at me once more.

"I'm only looking. I just want a quick peek!" I pouted.

Flipping my tail, I made my way slowly back to the soft dirt under the bushes. I could wait. Someday I would get a peek at what was making the curious noises in the nest.

All day Bird flew to the field and returned with juicy caterpillars and fluttery moths for her hungry family. Callie and I were able to move freely without worrying about Bird pecking us when we weren't expecting it. Papa Mockingbird still stood guard from the top of the pines but seemed to be watching for other enemies.

*　　*　　*

As the days passed, the noise from the nest grew louder, and I became more curious. I guess cats are just naturally curious. I had to see what was going on.

I waited until both birds flew off to the field. As soon as they were gone, I darted from under the bushes, climbed to the top of the logs, and started up the tree. The nest was resting in a crook on the first limb. Four tiny bird heads peeked back at me as I looked into the twig nest that Bird had made. They were weird! Their mouths were really big and yellow. Their feathers were kind of scraggly, making them look almost bald. Their skin was pink and their eyes were really round and—

Bird's beak hit me between the ears.

"Ouch!" I cried. "I was just looking!"

Before the *meow* even got out of my mouth, Bird pecked me again. She hit the middle of my neck, right between my shoulder blades. Off balance, I fell and landed on the woodpile. I didn't even take the time to wash my paws or sharpen my claws. I just jumped to the ground and ran.

"Gray Cat, I'm warning you! Stay away!"

Once I was safe under the pine trees, I stopped to clean my fur and get myself back together.

"Be careful, Birdies," I heard Bird warn her nest of pink babies. "Always be watching. Bad Cats are sneaky. They will come into the tree quietly and take you away. Cats like nothing better than to eat baby birds."

"I don't eat baby birds!" I argued, loud enough for them to hear. "Callie doesn't, either. She's too old to climb up the tree. I just wanted to see what was in your nest."

Bird gathered her babies under her wings.

"Don't believe him," she warned. "All cats chase birds."

"Not me," I meowed. "Honest!"

As I walked to the hayfield, I heard the loud noises from the nest. Bird took a swoop at me on her way to the pasture.

I glanced back at the tree. Papa Mockingbird glared at me from the top branches.

My tail flipped from side to side when I strutted toward the field. *A nice mouse will make me feel better,* I thought.

CHAPTER 3

The mice scurried as I strolled into the field. The House Daddy was working at the far end of the meadow with a big machine. The hay would soon be cut and, with no places left to hide, many of the mice would hurry to the creek or the rock hill for protection. Hunting was easy now, though.

I carried my trophy to the front yard. Callie was asleep on the porch swing. The House Mama came out the door just as I hopped up on the cool concrete.

"Gray! Yuck! Good kitty! Yuck! Take that mouse out to the field!" she yelled at me.

I smiled and headed for the mat to drop the mouse. Mama stamped her foot at me. Puzzled, I looked up. Maybe she didn't see the neat trophy in my mouth. I raised my head so she'd have a better view.

"See the prize I brought you," I purred.

She stamped the concrete again. "Get, Gray! Go away and take that thing with you!"

I was confused. I thought she would be proud of me, but here she was trying to shoo me away.

I swished my tail against her leg, and Mama picked me up. But she held me away from her. She usually held me close and petted me. I tried to turn so I could show her the trophy that I brought—just for her. At arm's length, she carried me to the end of the yard and set me down.

"Gray, I love you dearly, but please eat the mouse before you come to the porch!"

"I don't like the *whole* mouse," I purred. "I just like the crunchy part!" Mama didn't seem to understand my purrs. I tried to follow her back to the house. She kicked at me with her big paw—I mean, foot.

I finally dropped the trophy and gazed up at her. She smiled and walked away. She was almost to the house when Bird dropped out of the air and stabbed me in the back.

"Ouch!" I yowled. "That hurt!"

Mama turned around and started yelling at Bird. "Get away from Gray. Scat! Go on!"

Still chattering, Bird flew to the top of the pecan tree.

Satisfied that I was okay, Mama turned and walked to the door. She looked back again and stepped inside the house.

Bird started screaming at me as soon as the door closed. "Get out of here! Get away from my tree!"

Confused, I shook my head and looked around. "I'm not even close to your tree."

"Scat! Get away from here!" she screeched.

I flipped my tail, spun around, and trotted back to the porch. Callie's eyes opened when I jumped up beside her on the swing.

"This is getting ridiculous, Callie," I complained. "Why is Bird so upset?"

Callie stretched her neck and looked all around. "You got me, Gray! Why? What's happening?"

My tail gave a little jerk. "She pecked me and told me to get away from her tree."

Callie raised an eyebrow. "So?"

"I wasn't even close to her tree."

Callie frowned and looked around the yard once more. She shook her head, put it down on her paws, and closed her eyes. I folded my paws and lay down beside her.

"I don't think Bird likes me. I don't think she believes me, either."

"Believes you about what?" Callie asked, without opening her eyes.

"About not eating birds. I told her that I don't eat birds, but I don't think she believes me."

Callie peered at me out of one eye.

"That's okay. I don't believe you, either."

"But it's true," I whimpered.

Now Callie was staring at me with both eyes.

"All cats eat birds!" she argued. "We can't help ourselves. They flutter and wiggle and fluff around. We just *have* to pounce. We're cats."

I raised my chin off my paws. "I'm a cat, but I do *not* eat birds."

"Yeah, right!" Callie scoffed.

"Really!" I insisted.

Callie gave a curious frown. "Why?"

"When I was little," I began, "my brother and I sneaked out of the barn where we lived to explore the big world. We had just stepped into the sunlight for the very first time when we saw this bird.

"He didn't look at all like Bird. He walked around pecking at the ground. Instead of singing, he flapped his wings and said, 'Cock-a-doodle-doo!' The way he wiggled his feathers and strutted around made him look real interesting. My brother and I crept up on him. I pounced and tried to grab him with my teeth. Before I could blink, the big bird spun around and came after us. He clunked us on the heads with his wings. He kicked us with the sharp claws on his feet, and he pecked us with his hard beak. He did it so quickly that my brother and I didn't know what was happening. I had a mouthful of feathers that I swiped from him. His attack scared me so bad, I sucked them halfway down my throat.

"He chased us, pecked us, and clunked us all the way back to the barn. It hurt! But worst of all, I had those nasty feathers stuck in my throat. I coughed and spit and choked all night long.

"The next day I still had that awful taste and those fuzzy feathers stuck to the roof of my mouth. Mama said that roosters were mean. She said that she didn't ever mess with the rooster— and Mama was all grown-up. But whether he was mean or not didn't matter. I decided right then that I would never try to catch anything that was covered with yucky old feathers."

I sat up on my haunches and flipped my tail. "And I never have!"

Callie closed her eyes again and rested her chin on her paws. "I caught a bird or two, when I was younger. But I'm like you, I never cared too much for the feathers."

Suddenly Bird screamed and swooped down from the pecan tree. I flinched when I heard her zoom through the air. I was afraid she might be after me. She wasn't.

She flew up and down in the middle of the yard. I couldn't see what she was after at first.

So I stood up on the chair and stretched my neck as far as I could. It was the brown hose—I mean, Bullsnake.

"Why is she after Bullsnake?" I asked.

One of Callie's eyes popped open. She frowned, then stood up and stretched her neck like I had done. "Something is going on," she said. "Bullsnake never bothers anyone. He just wants to be left alone. He's clear out in the middle of the yard, and she's acting like she wants to tear him apart."

Callie hopped down from the porch. "I've got to go check this out." I followed her.

Sure enough, here came Bird. She swooped at us, then she swooped at Bullsnake. Then she swooped at us again, screaming as loud as she could each time she dived. I wanted to run back to the porch or hide in the holly bushes. Before I had the chance, Papa Mockingbird came after us, too.

He zoomed at us while Bird zoomed at Bullsnake. Then Bird pecked at us while Papa pecked at Bullsnake. I never heard so much swishing and screeching in my life. It was enough to make my tail fuzz.

It felt like the rooster attack when I was little. It filled my heart with terror!

CHAPTER 4

Callie scurried down the sidewalk. I stayed hot on her heels, ducking and flinching each time one of the birds made a fly-by. Once under the carport at the end of the sidewalk, we were safe from their attacks. But it didn't help the noise problem. The pair still kept screeching and screaming their threats at the top of their little bird lungs. To the right of the carport, on the other side of the chain-link fence, I could see the Mama. She was down on one knee, petting Muffy. She frowned when she looked over at us.

"Wonder what all the fuss is about?" she asked the old dog.

Callie nudged me with her shoulder.

"There's the problem," she said. "One of the baby birds has fallen from the nest."

I frowned, staring where Callie's nose was pointing.

"Where? What baby bird?"

"That little thing. There, beside the woodpile."

I tilted my head to the side. "He sure looks weird. He has even less feathers than I thought. The poor thing is almost naked."

Callie's sides jiggled in and out when she laughed. "It's a baby bird all right." She chuckled. "They don't get regular feathers until they're older."

"What are you laughing about?"

Callie shrugged her fur. "I just never heard anybody say a baby bird is naked."

"Well, it is!" I insisted. "And it's ugly, too. I never saw anything so ugly."

I trotted out for a closer look.

Big mistake.

When I walked out from under the carport, Bird stabbed me right in the middle of my back. It hurt so bad that I let out a loud meow. Before she could hit me again, I raced back for the safety of the roof.

The chain-link gate squeaked when Mama opened it. "What in the world is going on out here?" she asked, frowning down at me. "Between the bird squawking and you yowling, it sounds like a battle."

Folding her arms, she looked around.

"Oh, dear! No wonder they're making such a fuss." She shot me an angry glance. "I'd be upset, too, if some cat were trying to get my baby." She scurried off toward the fallen baby bird.

"I wasn't trying to get the bird. I was just looking!"

Mama didn't hear me. Either that or she just didn't understand. Very gently she picked up the baby bird and put it in the nest. When she came back, she shook a finger at me and Callie. "You two leave those birds alone."

"I didn't do anything," I protested. "I was just looking!"

Bird flew to her nest with a last warning. "Stay away from my nest! Leave my babies alone."

"I wasn't doing anything," I whined. "I was just looking!"

Now that the excitement was over, Callie curled up in a bed of pine needles to take a nap.

It was getting dark, so I decided to check if any mice were left in the field.

As I walked through the pasture I heard the distant sound of thunder. I would have to make a quick catch and be back before the rain came.

The field was nearly empty. Cut hay lay on the ground in rows. The mice must have moved to the rock hill. I leaped across a small creek to get to the rocky edge where the mice were hiding. I waited quietly, listening—watching for the slightest movement that would show me where they were. I flattened myself out and crawled along the edge of the hill.

The night seemed to be darker than usual. I heard a low rumble in the sky as I continued my search. Small drops of rain began to hit me on the back. I tried to shake them off. The raindrops got bigger. They were cold and wet. We cats don't like cold and wet. I scurried to hide under a rock ledge. The mice must have known that the storm was coming.

Wind shook the trees around me. Leaves fell to the ground as the lightning and thunder grew closer. Rain splashed the dirt, leaving small round dents where the big drops hit. I wanted to be back at the house. I wanted to be sitting safely on the rocking chair. Callie was probably asleep inside. She wouldn't even hear the wild sounds of the storm.

A bolt of lightning struck a tree on the hillside. My fur stood on end. I licked my shoulders trying to get it to lie down. Cracking sounds filled the air as the tree broke apart and fell to the ground. I pushed myself farther under the rock. Tucking my tail tight against my body, I knew that I would have to wait until the storm was over. I longed for the safety of the house and the people.

Small streams of water began running down the hillside. One ran near the rock cliff that I was tucked under. Limbs and twigs covered the ground as the wind gusts shook more of them loose from the trees. I was safe and dry under the cliff.

When I woke up from a small catnap, I could still hear thunder, but it was not as loud now. I wiggled out toward the edge of the rock over-hang. Peering up, I saw that a large branch had fallen onto the cliff that was protecting me. There was *stuff* everywhere. I had to twist and turn and squeeze and climb, just to get out of the tangled mess that the storm had left.

The creek was running high with murky water. I had to cross it, but it was deeper and wider than when I had come to the hillside. I followed the stream until I came to a sturdy branch that had fallen across it, making a bridge. Carefully I made my way over the rushing water.

The rows of hay in Daddy's field were all wet and soggy. The mice still weren't anywhere to be seen. I followed the path to the pasture in front of the house. I shook the drops of rain from my back as I listened for the sounds of scurrying mice. The stillness was finally broken by the squeal of a brown field mouse. I wiggled flat against the ground. My whiskers twitched. I glared at the big mouse.

Proudly I carried the trophy to the porch. The Mama would be impressed with a prize this big.

I could hardly wait until she found it on the mat. She would know that I was a great mouser when she saw this big one. I finished eating the crunchy part and headed for the rocking chair.

The usual glare from the yard light was missing. The storm must have knocked it out. The front porch was a mess. My rocking chair was turned over, and puddles of water covered the concrete. Limbs from the pecan tree littered the yard and wet leaves clung to everything. The corner of the porch was the only dry spot I could find, so I curled up for a nap.

Dreams of mice danced in my head until I heard the door open. The Mama was setting Callie down on the porch. The damage from the storm seemed to surprise Mama as she stepped outside.

I guess that she didn't look before she stepped. Her bare foot smushed the big, juicy mouse into the doormat. Suddenly the Mama began squealing and jumping around. "Gray, this is so gross!" She grabbed a broom and came after me.

I scurried past the front porch. "What's the matter?" I meowed as I shot out of her reach. "That is my best trophy yet! What did I do?"

I stopped at the end of the sidewalk. Washing my front paws, I carefully watched the Mama. She glared at me.

"Gray, why can't you just eat these nasty

things? I don't want them here where they stink up the place. This is awful!"

She was standing in the grass wiping off her bare foot. Maybe she should have been watching where she stepped. I always put my trophies on that mat. She should be proud of me. I was protecting the place from these creatures!

I washed my neck and headed for the woodpile. People were so hard to understand.

CHAPTER 5

Five weeks later there was another storm. It was even worse than the last one. This time, when the storm came, I got to go inside the house with Callie. It was lots better than hiding under the ledge on the rock hill.

Lots of changes had happened since the last storm. The little, naked birds had gotten their feathers. One at a time they had climbed out on the limb where their nest was and practiced flopping their wings. Bird and Papa Mockingbird were so busy feeding their babies, they didn't bother Callie, me, or even Bullsnake very much.

One day one of the babies jumped from a limb and tried to fly. Only he didn't make it very far. He landed in the middle of the yard. Callie and

I hid from Papa Mockingbird until the baby managed to fly back up into the tree.

Lately, every bird but one had been flying. They weren't as good as Bird and Papa Mockingbird, but they were flying all over the place. A couple were even starting to catch their own food.

All except one bird.

I didn't know what the problem was with that one, but it never left the nest. It didn't climb out on the limb and flap its wings. It just sat in the pile of twigs looking scared and nervous.

I watched out the front window, but I couldn't see any of the birds. I was glad when Mama opened the front door to let Callie and me out. I could hardly wait to investigate. Things were always different after a storm.

The yard was covered with twigs and branches. Needles littered the ground around the tall pine trees. Grasshoppers moved slowly as the sunshine spread through the branches.

I sat on my haunches and watched the apple tree. None of the birds were around. Papa Mockingbird was no place to be seen, and none of the babies flapped their wings or practiced flying from one tree to the next. The nest looked empty.

Suddenly I heard something flutter. Bird

swooped down from a pine tree. She grabbed one of the grasshoppers, who was sunning itself on a lilac leaf. With a bug in her beak she flew to one of the branches that held her nest. But instead of going to the pile of twigs, she stood far out on the limb.

She waited there a long time. Finally a gray fuzzy head popped up from inside the nest. "I'm hungry," it chirped.

"I'm not bringing you any more food," Bird mumbled.

(It was hard to understand her because she had a beak full of grasshopper.)

"If you want something to eat, you'll have to come out here and get it!"

Cautiously the baby Mockingbird hopped to the edge of the nest. Wings out for balance, she jumped to the limb where Bird stood. One step at a time she eased her way toward her mother. But just as she reached out to take the grasshopper, Bird dropped it.

"Oops," Bird said. "Fly down and get him. Quick! Fly after him before he gets away."

The baby Mockingbird looked down at the ground. Then she turned, hopped sideways along the limb, and disappeared into the nest.

Bird began to cry.

My sharp ears pointed forward. I frowned, watching her for a time, then walked to the woodpile. Bird didn't fly or swoop at me when I got near, so I climbed to the top of the logs. Bird still didn't come after me.

"Hey Bird, what's wrong?"

She sighed. Her feathers drooped. "Oh, it's her." Bird sniffed. "All my other babies learned to fly just like they were supposed to. They have already left the nest. Even Papa Mockingbird has taken off on his journey south for the winter. Very soon I will have to leave, too. But she won't fly. She won't even leave the nest."

I stretched my neck trying to see inside the pile of twigs. "Is she sick? Maybe she's hurt. Maybe that's why she won't fly."

Bird ruffled her feathers.

"No! She's strong and healthy. She just won't try her wings."

Bird looked so sad, it made me feel sad, too.

"Is there anything I can do?"

Bird glared down her pointed beak at me. "You're a cat! I'll stay long enough to feed her one more day, then I must leave. If she doesn't fly away with me, you'll probably eat her. That's what cats do."

"I don't eat birds," I told her, but she didn't listen. She wiped a tear from under her eye with one of her wing feathers. Then she flew away and began gathering moths and caterpillars to bring back to the nest.

I felt very sad. After a time on the woodpile I had to find someplace to go. I had to find something to do to take my mind off the sad feeling I had inside.

My tail flipped when I glanced at the barn. The last time I tried to check there, the big wood doors were closed. I licked my lips. I wondered if there were any mice in the barn.

The doors were open just a crack. But there was enough space to stick my head in. My whiskers didn't even touch, so I knew there was plenty of room for the rest of me to fit through. Quiet as could be, I slipped inside. It was dark. I stood by the door a second until my eyes got used to the dim shadows.

The barn was really big. The walls were made of metal and the roof was metal, too. There were big wooden boards running across the top of the barn to hold the roof up. Other poles and boards came down the sides to hold the walls. There was hay inside, too. I recognized the smell, but it didn't look like the hay in the field. This hay was all clumped together in big square chunks. I think the House Daddy called them bales. They were piled—one on top of the other—along the sides and at the corners of the barn.

To my left was an open room. There was no hay inside, not even any pieces scattered about.

There was just a big concrete floor, with a black stain right in the middle.

Another smell made my whiskers wiggle. It was a familiar odor, only I couldn't quite put my claw on it. Frowning, I looked around. There was something in the corner. My sharp cat eyes narrowed, trying to make it out. Suddenly they flashed wide.

It was a mouse—but *what a mouse!* The thing was huge! It looked like a mouse. It smelled like a mouse. But I had never seen such a *big* mouse. It was chewing on some little yellow chunks of grain. I swished my tail and flattened my ears.

What a trophy! If I brought this to the mat, Mama couldn't help but be proud of me. Even if she forgot to look and stepped on it barefoot, she'd still be excited and impressed. I bet she wouldn't even yell at me.

Inch at a time, I crept toward it. I kept low. Just a few more feet and I would be close enough to pounce.

Suddenly I got this weird feeling. It kind of tingled the fur on the back of my neck. It made me feel strange—as if someone was watching me. I stopped. Looked around.

Another giant mouse glared down at me from the top of a haybale. His beady eyes never blinked as he sat licking his lips.

Two giant mouses. The Mama wouldn't believe her eyes. She would know I was the best mouser in the world if . . .

The little scratchy sound behind me made me whirl around. Now there were three. A huge mouse had appeared between me and the door. Crouching close to the ground, he glared at me with beady yellow eyes. It made the hair on my back stand up. It was a weird feeling, like my hair was crawling and got stuck up in a sharp ridge down my spine. My tail jerked back and forth, all by itself. It was like I had no control of it.

"Hey, Cat." The giant mouse on top of the hay bale sneered. "What do you think you're doing in my barn?"

"Your barn? Mice don't have barns. It doesn't belong to you. I thought this was the House People's barn." My tail flipped again. Quickly I sat on it so they wouldn't see how nervous I was.

He grinned and licked his lips.

"I'm not a mouse." He smiled. "I'm a rat!"

"A rat? What's a rat?"

The one behind me moved closer.

"Rats are big. Rats are very smart. And rats are always . . ."

"Rats are always what?" I tried to get him to finish what he was telling me.

The one on the hay jumped to the floor of the barn. His teeth glistened when he glanced toward

the other big mouse who was eating the yellow grain. "Hey, Nora," he whispered, "look what we got here."

The one he called Nora dropped the piece of grain she was munching and moved toward me. Her eyes were small and beady. When she smiled, her lips curled. She had big, *long* yellow teeth.

"Ooooh." She licked her lips. "A little kitty cat."

"Rats are always what?" I asked again.

All three mice—I mean rats—moved toward me. They came closer and closer. The ridge of hair that stood up on my back went clear down to the tip of my tail now. All fuzzed up, it was so big that it was almost impossible for me to sit on it. I eased to my feet. My tail shot straight up in the air behind me. It was nearly as big around as the rest of me.

The huge rats moved closer. One stood between me and the door. On trembling legs, I took a step back. The one named Nora licked her lips again.

"Rats are big. Rats are smart." Her eyes seemed to sparkle. "And rats are always . . . *hungry*."

I couldn't hold still. My legs took off. I ran!

At the far corner of the barn was a pile of hay. That didn't stop me. I scampered up the bales of hay. I got as far away from the huge rats as I could.

My legs shook so hard, I could barely stand. I shoved myself into the corner of the barn, panting and gasping for air. The rats were no place in sight. But I could hear them—somewhere—they were giggling and laughing at me.

A puff of red exploded in front of my eyes. "You're a cat!" I growled to myself. "Cats aren't afraid of mice. Cats aren't afraid of rats. Cats eat rats for snacks. What's wrong with you? Get down from this stack of hay and go get 'em!"

I took a deep breath and stepped out from the corner. *I'm a cat*, I thought. *I can do this. . . .*

"Here, kitty, kitty, kitty."

The voice came from above me. Eyes wide, I looked up. One of the rats stood on a wood rafter, just over my head. My bottom bumped the tin wall when I backed into the corner once more.

A sharp, pointy nose appeared over the bale of hay where I stood. Nora's beady eyes followed.

"There you are. I thought we lost you for a second." She smiled and licked her lips once more. "Here, kitty, kitty, kitty."

I was trapped like a rat . . . I mean, like a cat. The huge rats had me pinned in the corner. They had me surrounded. There was no escape.

CHAPTER 6

I meowed and hissed as loud as I could. I raised my paw and my claws sprang out. It was no use.

The third rat appeared at my left. I shivered. This wasn't the way it was supposed to be. Cats are supposed to eat rats. Rats aren't supposed to eat cats! The instant Nora climbed to the top of my hay bale, I took off again.

As she pulled herself over the edge, I leaped from the pile of hay. She snapped at me, her long yellow teeth just missing my leg. The hay was so high, I had to wave my paws and swing my tail to keep my balance. When I hit the floor, it knocked the wind out of me. I stumbled, but scrambled to my feet once more. Fast as I could, I raced for the other side of the barn. There was no hay there, so I backed into the corner. Watched. Waited.

Nora hopped down and hurried across the floor. The big rat, on the wood rafters at the top of the barn, scurried toward me, too. Frantic, I looked all around. I couldn't find the third rat.

"Hey," a voice called. "Who's up there. Who's jumping around on my roof?"

Suddenly another pointy nose appeared out of a hole. It was so close that I could see his black eyes squinting at me. He blinked.

"What's going on up there?"

"Hey, Smitty," Nora called in her squeaky rat voice. "It's a kitty cat. He's on the roof of your rat hole. Help us get him cornered."

The eyes blinked. The pointy nose wiggled.

"Oh, boy. Fresh meat."

A single strip of light shone through the opening between the two doors. It made the hay shiny green and brought a brightness to the dreary, frightening barn. Nora blocked my path, but it was my only chance.

I ran straight for Nora. At the last second she squeaked and jumped aside. I dodged in the other direction, slid a tiny bit on the loose hay, then shot through the opening between the two doors. I didn't stop running until I was safe beside Callie on the porch swing.

Callie raised up and looked at me, but she didn't say anything. That was okay because I was breathing so hard that I probably couldn't have

heard her, anyway. It took a while for my hair to unfuzz. It took even longer for my legs to quit shaking and for me to breathe without wheezing and rasping.

"Want to talk about it?" the old cat finally asked.

I took a deep breath. A little shudder raced through me, so I took another breath.

"I went in the barn. And . . . and . . ."

"Met the rats, huh?"

I nodded, digging my claws into the swing to keep the shudders from shaking me again. "They chased me. They were gonna eat me!"

Callie made a little snorting sound and put her head back on her paws. "I bet the reason they chased you was because you ran. Rats are cowards. They won't even take a kitten like you on in a fair fight. Probably at least three or four of them, right?"

"Four. They were big, too. Really big!"

Callie nodded. "Like I said, they run in gangs. Only cowards run in gangs. If you hadn't run from them . . ."

"You mean, they wouldn't have done anything to me if I hadn't run from them?"

Callie raised her head. Her whiskers twitched from side to side. "Hard to tell. You're not a kitten anymore, but you're not a full-grown cat, either. You can't always figure out what rats are going to do. But, like I said, they're cowards. Usually, they won't fight a cat. Not even a young, small cat like you. Still . . . well . . . probably would be a good idea if you stayed out of the barn until you're a little bigger."

"I don't think I'll ever go back in the barn," I said, shaking my head. "Not ever again."

Callie only smiled.

"You will. Cats hate rats."

"Why?"

"Well, rats are destroyers. They eat or gnaw or tear up all our people's things. We cats love our people. We can't put up with rats making our people miserable or hurting their stuff. It's just the way we are."

"When will I be big? When will I *not be afraid* of rats?"

"You'll know," Callie said. "You'll know."

With that, Callie kissed me between the eyes. She washed and cleaned my forehead with her rough tongue. Then she washed behind my ears. After a while I didn't feel so scared anymore. I felt like a baby kitten again with Mama loving me and taking care of me. Before I knew it, I fell asleep.

Catnaps always make us cats feel better. When I woke up, I strolled straight to the door of the barn. My eyes narrowed. I felt mean and strong and . . .

"Here, kitty, kitty, kitty," a voice called from inside.

I stopped running when I got to the woodpile. Okay—so they looked like mice. But I never saw such big mice—I mean, rats. I never saw such long teeth. I could explore the barn—later. Maybe when I was bigger and stronger.

It was three days before I got the nerve to go near the barn. I wasn't bigger or stronger—at least not yet—but I was a cat! Cats aren't afraid of mice, even big ones like rats. Although I was a tiny bit scared, I knew that I would have to face them.

The woodpile was as close as I got to the barn. I watched and waited from there for any signs of the ugly rats. Suddenly a gentle thump hit me on the head. It wasn't as sharp as Bird's beak. It didn't sting, then go away, only to swoop back and sting again. But something was there. Something was on my head!

CHAPTER 7

Eat me."

"What?"

"Eat me!"

"Who said that?" I looked up. That's where the voice came from. But I couldn't see anything. I twisted my neck to the side. Still nothing. I flipped my back end around trying to find who was speaking to me.

"Cat, I'm up here. On your head."

I waved my ears. I wiggled my whiskers.

There was something on my head, all right. I could feel it. It was not very heavy, but something was there! Sharp needles kind of scratched my skull. Almost cross-eyed, I looked up again.

A small, pointed, feathered head peeked down. Beady bird eyes blinked.

"Get off my head!"

"Okay—if you'll eat me."

"No."

The beady bird eyes blinked again. The corners of the beak wiggled down to a frown.

"What do you mean, no?"

"No means *no!* I don't eat birds."

The feathered head cocked to the side. "But cats eat birds, don't they?"

"Well . . . yes . . . I guess. Most cats do. But I don't eat birds. Now get off."

"What do you mean, you don't eat birds?"

"Well, when I was little I was attacked by a mad rooster. I don't like feathers in my mouth, and the rooster was so big and mean and frightening that—"

"Look, Cat," the bird interrupted. "I don't want your life history. I just want to get it over with."

I lay down and flopped over on my side. Maybe I could knock her off. Only when I rolled over, she just clung to me. When I lay on my side, she walked to the other side of my head. When I rolled to my back, she walked to my face. She stood right on my mouth and glared me in the eye.

"Get what over with?" I mumbled. (I mumbled because it was hard to talk with a bird standing on my mouth.)

"I can't fly." She pouted. "All my family went south for the winter, and I'm here—all alone. I don't want to starve. Mama told us that cats eat birds, so I figured . . . well . . . it's quicker than starving to death."

I shook my head. Her little claws clamped harder to my mouth. She was starting to smush my whiskers. I flipped over so I could get my paws under me. She walked around my head as I rolled. By the time I stood up, she was perched between my ears again.

"Look, bird. I wish I could help you, but—"

"Just my luck," she chirped. "I'm starving to death, and I land on the only cat in the country who won't eat birds. If you won't eat me, then feed me!"

"What?"

"I'm hungry. Get me something to eat!"

"What? You're a bird!"

"Look. We've already been through that. I'm a bird. You're a cat. Only you don't eat birds. Either eat me or feed me. *I'm hungry!*"

I twitched my whiskers, thinking for a moment. "Well, there's some cat food inside. I didn't eat all of it this morning. I guess I could take you in there and—" I broke off what I was saying when a sudden vision flashed through my head. I could just see me, marching into the People house with a bird on my head. I was a cat! What was I thinking?

"Bird, you are going to have to get off my head," I yowled.

"Feed me first."

"I'm a cat. I can't go around with a bird on my head. Get off!"

"Nope. Not until I get something to eat."

"I need to hunt and take catnaps each day. I can't go around with a silly, little bird on my head. *Get off!*" I growled deep in my throat.

The bird tightened her grip. "No."

"Will you get off if I find you something to eat?"

The bird didn't answer.

"Will you?"

"Look, Cat, I really am hungry. Can you get me a snack? I haven't eaten since yesterday. Mama always brings a nice breakfast as soon as the sun comes up. But today she didn't come back."

"What does she bring you?"

"Well, Cat, she brings moths or caterpillars or—"

"Listen, you. My name is Gray. Quit calling me Cat."

"Okay, Gray. She brings caterpillars and moths or grasshoppers."

"Look . . . uh . . . what do I call you?"

"Mama called us all Birdies. You can call me whatever you want," the bird chirped.

"How about Pest?" I asked.

"I don't care. If you get me something to eat, you can call me anything you want. Just feed me!"

"Okay . . . Pest is a little too much. How about Flea? I had a flea once, and he was as hard to get rid of as you are."

She cocked her head to one side.

"Flea is a great name. Now, please get me something to eat."

"I can't think with a bird on my head. Would you please move to my neck or back?" I flattened my body on the ground, hoping that the bird would move.

"Okay. Just remember that you promised to feed me. You have to feed me or eat me, okay?" Flea moved to my neck, then to my back.

I could still feel those tiny claws moving around, but somehow they didn't seem to be as bad as when she was on my head.

I tried to figure out how I was going to feed this little bird. Birds don't eat mice. I saw plenty of moths flying around the yardlight at night, but they were always up high in the air. And caterpillars . . . well, just the thought of catching one of those wiggly, little crawly things . . .

"Hey, Flea, do you like grasshoppers?" I asked,

remembering the ones that I had seen this morning.

"Mama brings them to us sometimes. They're not my favorites, but I *am* hungry."

I walked toward the yard where I had seen the bugs. They didn't seem to be as slow, now that the sun was up. I spotted a small, thin one on a blade of grass. I crouched and moved slowly toward it. Inching up, I watched it carefully. I pounced. Got it!

I twisted my head around so the bird could take it. "Here, Flea." I mumbled because I had a grasshopper hanging out the side of my mouth.

Little bird feet moved toward my head. Suddenly they stopped.

"I can't reach it. I'll fall off."

"So?" I mumbled. "If you fall off, get back on."

"No. You'll have to throw it to me."

I took a deep breath and sighed. This wasn't going to be easy. I tossed the grasshopper over my shoulder. It landed in the grass. Flipping around, I pounced and grabbed it again. I tried the toss once more, but Flea missed. Being a determined cat, I tossed it over and over and over until it finally landed on my back.

Flea gobbled it down. "I'm hungry," she chirped as soon as she had eaten the small insect.

I spent the next twenty minutes hopping around the yard like an idiot, pouncing on grasshoppers. I got better at tossing them onto my back. When Flea finally quit her demands for more food, we walked to the porch for a catnap.

"Nice bird." Callie grinned from her rocking chair.

"Yeah, thanks. Got any ideas to help me?" I twitched my ears.

Callie looked back sleepily. "Sure, you could have a morning snack."

I flopped down on the cool concrete. "You know I don't eat birds."

Callie shrugged and closed her eyes. "I don't have any other ideas, but you *do* look pretty silly with a bird on your back."

Flea was being very quiet. I could still feel her small claws. I looked around, trying to see what she was doing.

The pesky bird had nestled down into my fur—and was fast asleep!

It made me shudder. What was I going to do with a stupid bird on my back? Cats don't go around with hitchhiking birds—it's just not natural. I sighed, crossed my paws, and put my cheek on them. Maybe things would be better after a nice nap.

CHAPTER 8

After some time and practice, my tossing got much better. Flea's catching improved, too. We could get that bird fed in just a few minutes. I had some trouble with my mouse-catching, though.

As soon as I crept into the hayfield, and the mice spotted the bird on my back, they started laughing. Now, it should be easy to catch a giggling mouse. But somehow it was embarrassing to have your snacks laugh at you.

"Flea, you are going to have to hide down in my fur," I moaned. "These mice aren't taking me seriously."

"Take your time, Gray. Look them in the eye. When they see that you mean business, they won't laugh at you!" Good advice from a parasite bird.

Flea tucked herself into my fur and the chase began. I looked those mice in the eye, and sure enough it was no time at all before I had a trophy to take back to the house.

As we walked past the woodpile, Flea began grabbing and tugging on my fur.

"Gray! There's the snake!" she cheeped.

"So?"

I looked at the woodpile. Curled up near the bottom of the tree was the snake. He raised his head. Clinging to my hair, Flea began to bounce up and down.

"Hurry, Gray! Get away!"

"That's just Bullsnake."

"But Mama warned me about Snake. She said that snakes are as bad as cats when it comes to eating baby birds."

I rolled my eyes to look up at her. "I thought you wanted to be eaten. That's what you kept saying yesterday—'Eat me!' "

"That was yesterday when I was starving. Now that my tummy is full, I don't want to be eaten."

I started to explain to Flea that Bullsnake wouldn't bother her. All he wanted was to be left alone, but Snake had already disappeared under the logs, so I didn't bother.

"Let's see what's going on at the house."

I hurried to the porch and put my trophy on

the mat. When I jumped up onto the rocking chair, Callie looked up at us from the concrete.

"I see that you still have your little snack on your back," she purred.

"We've been hunting for mice."

"It won't be long before it gets cold." Callie winced when she stretched out her paws.

"How do you know?" I asked.

"Arthritis." Callie flinched again when she arched her back. "My old bones and joints get kind of sore when a cold front is coming in."

I glanced at the front door. "Does the Mama let you in when it gets cold?"

"Yes."

"Do you think she'll let me come in, too?"

"Yes, I think so."

I smiled. "No problem. I will enjoy spending more time in the house. It makes me almost look forward to winter."

"But you do have one little problem," Callie said. She didn't look me in the eye when she spoke. I felt my eyes roll upward, trying to follow her glance.

"Oh, yeah! I almost forgot. Do you think the Mama will let her come in, too?"

Callie shot me a disgusted look.

"How about the barn?" I suggested.

Callie rolled her eyes. "The rats would love that."

My whiskers twitched. "Surely we can find somewhere warm for her to spend the winter."

Callie rested her chin on her crossed paws. "Even if you could find a warm place for her to spend the winter, what would she eat? There aren't any bugs. Even the earthworms go deep into the ground. Your bird cannot spend the winter here. Birds fly south for the winter. That's just how things are."

I twisted my neck as far as I could. Flea was nestled down into my fur and fast asleep. "But she can't fly!" I whispered.

"Is she hurt?" Callie asked.

"No."

"Is she sick?"

"No. I think she's just scared. She fell out of her nest when she was very little, and ever since she's been afraid of heights. Her little wings are very strong. I can feel them when she flaps on my back."

Callie sighed and shook her head.

"Your little Flea must fly south for the winter. If she won't fly, then she will die."

"What can *I* do? I don't know how to fly."

Callie shrugged. Then, she closed her eyes and went to sleep. But I couldn't go to sleep. All I could do was lie there and wonder how I could help this pesky Flea.

*   *   *

We spent the afternoon with a flying lesson. I ran across the yard. Flea flapped her little wings. She hopped up and tried to catch the wind, but each time Flea fell back on me. Hop and flutter, Flea tried again and again to fly. I flattened my ears against my head and ran as fast as I could. We raced up and down the yard for hours. Exhausted, I tumbled to the concrete porch. We'd try again after a nap.

A scratching on my back woke me up—Flea was pecking and grabbing at me.

"Gray! Look out! There's that snake again."

I opened my eyes wide. The brown snake was crawling across the yard toward the woodpile. He stopped and looked back at us. I jumped up on the rocking chair to get a better view. Bullsnake gave a quiet hiss and crawled on toward the woodpile.

"He's trying to get me! Mama warned me about snakes," the little bird cheeped.

"You're safe with me. I'll take care of you," I meowed.

"I've got to learn how to fly . . . quick!" Flea sounded desperate.

We spent another hour fluttering and hopping, running and flapping before we finally went to the field for a quick snack. I caught a few grass-

hoppers for Flea and a couple of field mice for me. I even took a trophy home to put by the front door.

The House Mama found it as soon as she stepped out. Now, she always looked at the mat before walking out onto the porch—especially if she didn't have her shoes on. When she came outside, I flattened myself against the wall. If Mama saw me, she might try to give me a tummy rub. That would be very nice, but I was afraid that she would toss Flea into the yard like she did my trophies. So I tried to disappear into the brick behind the swing.

Mama called Callie and finally found her behind the rosebushes. She picked her up carefully and carried her inside. Flea was safe for today.

"Hey, Flea. We have to find some way for you to get off my back for just a little while. I need a good tummy rub from the Mama." I suddenly missed those rubs that I got from her.

"Find me some dirt to dig in, Gray," Flea chirped. "I could use a nice juicy worm. Those grasshoppers are very dry."

I went to the flower garden in the backyard where I had seen the dog digging. The dirt was soft there. Muffy was sound asleep, in a patch of sunlight, at the far side of the yard.

"I'm not worried about sliding off, but how will I get back on?" Flea moaned.

"We'll come up with something."

Carefully the bird let go and plopped quietly onto the soft dirt.

"I'll be right back, Flea."

I shook my whole body as I walked back to the front porch. "MEOW!" I yelled at the top of my voice. I had to get my tummy rubbed. "MEOOW!" I repeated. Finally I reached my front paws up to the middle of the screen door. I stretched out my claws and scratched the screen. I made as much noise as I could. It didn't take long before I heard the Mama coming.

"Gray, where have you been?" Mama reached down and picked me up. She sat on the swing and petted me. She started with my ears and chin, then my back and tail. I was feeling quite sleepy by the time she finished with my tummy.

"It's late, Gray. I have to go in." She set me down on the rocker and walked to the door. With a gentle smile she closed it behind her.

Suddenly I remembered Flea and hurried to the backyard.

The old dog was still asleep in the far corner.

"What took you so long, Gray? I've been finished with my hunt for a long time."

"Sorry, Mama's tummy rub felt better than I thought. I had to let her finish." Just remembering made me purr.

"Get me out of here, that snake could show

up anytime. He might be able to smell my fluffy feathers.''

I flattened myself down on the dirt. Flea took a big hop and fluttered her wings. I could feel her sharp claws grab my fur.

Hop and flutter. Hop and flutter. Each day Flea got better. She really improved when I stopped catching her food. I was totally sneaky about the way I did it, too.

When it came to catching grasshoppers, I pretended to get clumsy. I kept pouncing, only I would miss every time. Finally Flea told me to get close to the grasshoppers, then stop. She could jump on them. Each time I stopped farther from the grasshoppers. It wasn't long before Flea would swoop from my back and grab one. As soon as she gobbled it down, she hopped, gave a flap of her wings, and zoomed back to my head.

Flea really could fly. She just didn't know it—not yet.

Chapter 9

When Flea was asleep on my back, Callie jumped down from the rocking chair and eased over beside me. "How are the flying lessons coming?" she whispered.

"She's doing great!" I was careful not to move or disturb Flea. "She's flying and catching grasshoppers now. The only trouble is, she never gets more than six inches off the ground."

Callie glanced at my back. "Have you tried putting her up in the tree?"

"Tried that day before yesterday. She wouldn't leave the branch."

"Did you try pushing her off? I've seen other mama birds do that with their babies."

"Yes." I nodded, then gave a disgusted sigh. "She just hung on, and when we got to the tip of the branch, she ended up holding on to the bottom of the limb. She looked like a stupid bat hanging upside-down. She really *can* fly. She just won't."

Callie wiggled her whiskers. "I believe you. I was watching you two the other day, when she was chasing the grasshoppers. She's really pretty good. Maybe she just needs more confidence."

I frowned. "What does that mean?"

"What does what mean?"

"That confidence thing. What is it?"

"Well," Callie began as she nibbled on her bottom lip. "You know that Flea can fly. I know that Flea can fly. Flea just doesn't know that she can fly. She still thinks she is going to fall and hurt herself like she did when she fell out of her nest. We have to figure out some way to make her believe in herself."

"But how?"

For the next couple of days that was all Callie and I thought about. Flea was a bird who could fly but wouldn't fly more than six inches off the ground. The two of us had to figure some way to make Flea believe in herself. No matter how hard we tried, we just couldn't figure out how to do it. Until . . .

* * *

"You're getting too close to the woodpile!" Flea dug her little bird claws into my back and started bouncing up and down. Then she scampered to my head and began bouncing up and down there.

I went way around the woodpile. Callie was smiling when we got to the porch. "Gray, why don't you take Flea and put her in the redbud tree on the other side of the house. The wind is blowing from that direction. Maybe if she feels the air flowing under her wings, she will try to fly."

"No way!" Flea clutched tighter. "I'll sit in the tree, but there is no way that I will jump out of something that high."

"I told you so," I whispered to Callie.

"Try it anyway," Callie said. Then she gave me a quick wink.

I climbed halfway up the redbud tree and made Flea get off. I left her there, then went to see what Callie was up to. She was at the far end of the sidewalk when I got back. With a jerk of her head she motioned me to follow her.

"What's going on?" I asked when I caught up with her. "Why are we headed to the woodpile?"

"I've got an idea how we can get Flea to fly. But we're going to need Bullsnake's help. It's not going to be easy."

When we got to the woodpile, we looked underneath the logs. We looked between the logs. It was dark and hard to see, but there was no sign of Bullsnake. Suddenly, from a dark shadow, we heard a soft hiss.

"Leave me alone."

Callie's tail jerked. "Bullsnake, is that you?"

"Leave me alone," he hissed again.

"We need your help with Gray's little bird. Please."

"No! Leave me alone. Get away from my woodpile before the people see you."

I tapped Callie with my paw. "What's the deal with the people seeing us?" Why should that bother him?

"If the people see you hanging around my woodpile"—it was the hiss who answered instead of Callie—"they might find out that I am here. Please go away. Leave me alone."

I leaned close to Callie's ear. "Why doesn't he want the people to know?" I whispered very softly so that Snake wouldn't hear.

"Most snakes are okay," Callie explained. "They don't bother people or even us cats. They eat mice. In fact, if it wasn't for Bullsnake, I would never have been able to keep up with the mouse problem around here. There would be so many mice, there wouldn't be room for the people.

"But some snakes are very, very bad. They are

poisonous. If they bite a cat, they can kill. If they bite people, they can make them very sick. Trouble is, most House People don't know the difference between good snakes and bad snakes. They think all snakes are bad. When they find one, they look around for a big rock or a hoe so that they get rid of them. I don't blame Snake for being afraid."

Callie leaned down to peek under the logs. "We really do need your help. Pretty please!"

"Leave me alone!"

I nudged Callie with my shoulder, smiled, and licked my whiskers.

"Mr. Bullsnake," I began politely, "we *will* leave you alone if you promise to help us. But if you don't help us we'll stay here all day. Callie will meow. I'll climb on top of the woodpile. We will both make so much racket, the House People will have to notice us. When they come out we will show them where you live!"

Callie winked at me and nodded her head. She leaned down to peek under the woodpile. "If you help us, we'll leave you alone. We promise."

A forked tongue stuck out at us. Slowly and carefully a brown head appeared from under the logs.

"You promise that you'll leave me alone?"

"We promise!" both of us answered at the same time.

"I don't like it, but all right. What do I have to do?"

Callie sat down and wrapped her tail around her legs. "Okay, Snake, here's the plan. . . ."

CHAPTER 10

The next morning Flea and I headed out early for the field. There were a lot of mice scurrying around, but there weren't many grasshoppers. I guess, like Callie, they could tell that another big cold front was on the way. It took a long time to get Flea's breakfast, but it was easy for me to find a trophy for the mat.

I told Flea that I wanted to see if Mama would give me a tummy rub. I took her to a limb on the pecan tree and told her to wait there until Mama came out.

"Are you sure about this?" I asked Callie while we waited on the porch.

"I'm sure. Saturday is always grocery day. We have to wait until she leaves, otherwise it wouldn't be fair to Bullsnake."

It seemed as if we waited forever. At long last Mama came out of the front door. When she saw the trophy on the mat, she patted me on the head and said, "Good kitty." Then, as usual, she said, "Yuck," and threw my trophy into the yard. Just like Callie promised, Mama went down the sidewalk and got into her car. It groaned and growled when she tried to start it. Finally, after three times, it roared, sputtered, and chugged down the driveway.

Once she was gone, I glanced at Callie. She nodded.

I made a big show when I stood up, stretched, and arched my back. "I feel kind of stiff this morning," I meowed loudly.

"Sounds like you need a little catnap in the sun," Callie said, making sure that her meow was loud, too.

"Good idea."

I strolled out to the driveway and found a nice spot where there was plenty of sunshine. I curled up for my nap. It was *really* hard to keep my eyes closed. But no matter how badly I wanted to peek, I forced them to stay shut.

A scraping sound on the gravel came to my ears. The closer it got, the harder I squeezed my eyes.

"Gray. Gray! Wake up!" The loud, shrill, frightened shriek came from the pecan tree.

I didn't move. I didn't even twitch my whiskers or my tail. The scraping sound came closer. My eyes were closed tight. The noise from the little rocks clicking together stopped.

"This is the dumbest idea I've ever heard," a voice hissed. "It will never work."

"Quit griping," I whispered back. I struggled to stay still. "Just do it."

"Gray! Wake up quick!" This time the chirping that came from the tree was a scream.

"Ready?" I asked.

"Ready."

"Gray! Run! Get up! You have to get away!" Flea chirped as loud as she could.

With my eyes still closed, I raised my head and yawned. I opened my eyes. The second I opened them, I forced my eyes as big and round as I could. That's the way we had planned it—only my eyes got a lot bigger than I ever imagined.

All coiled up, Bullsnake looked *HUGE!* I sprang to my feet. Every muscle inside of me wanted to run. Even standing, Bullsnake's head still towered above me. I took a step backward. His forked tongue darted out. I backed away once more. Quicker than I could blink, Bullsnake scooted closer. He was right in my face.

This time I sort of leaped back. But when I did, I bumped into something—the woodpile. Bullsnake darted toward me again. He opened his mouth. The loud hiss that came out was ugly and frightening. I felt my fur fuzz. He dug the tip of his tail down into the gravel, and shook it as fast and hard as he could. Suddenly I realized that I really was scared.

I hissed back at him. I raised a paw. My claws sprang out.

"Watch it," he hissed. "You're supposed to look scared, remember."

I blinked a couple of times and got myself under control. Crouching low, I pushed back against the woodpile.

"Help me, help me!" I cried.

Nothing happened. Snake hissed again. I pushed myself harder against the logs.

"Help me! Snake has me trapped. He's going to bite me."

Still, nothing.

Bullsnake took a deep breath. It made him look even bigger than before. He raised his head higher. He opened his mouth wider.

"I've got you now, Gray Cat! I'm going to eat you for breakfast."

Zoom! From the tree came the flutter of wings. *Thunk!* Flea smacked into the side of Bull-snake's head.

"Ouch," Snake hissed. "That hurt!"

Flea swooped high into the air. "Run, Gray. Get away. Quick!" She dived at him again. She

pecked him on the back this time. "Leave my friend alone, you nasty, evil old snake!"

The moment Flea hit Bullsnake the third time, I darted away from the woodpile. Ears and whiskers flat against my face, I raced to the front porch. Flea swooped at Bullsnake again. She pecked the end of his tail, really hard, as it disappeared under the logs.

"Man, that one hurt!" His voice sounded funny from underneath all the wood.

Flea flew to the very top of the apple tree. She perched there for a moment, to make sure Bullsnake was still under the woodpile. Then she flew back to the pecan tree.

"Gray, are you okay? You're not hurt, are you?"

I licked my shoulder and looked myself over. "I think I'm okay. What happened? I . . . I don't remember. Bullsnake was about to get me, then . . . then . . . Callie? Was it you? Did you save me?"

Purring, Callie shook her head.

"No. I couldn't get there in time. It was Flea. She saved you."

I looked up in the pecan tree. It was hard not to smile.

"But how? How did she save me from the snake? How did she get there—in time?"

Callie switched her tail from side to side. She took a deep breath.

"She flew!"

"She what?"

"She flew. She *flew* from the pecan tree and pecked the snake on top of the head. Then she *flew* at him again and again until you were able to get away. Flea did it all by herself. Her wonderful flying skills saved you."

Both of us looked up in the pecan tree. Flea frowned at us. Then she blinked her little bird eyes. For a moment she looked downright confused. Then she blinked again and seemed almost startled. She held her wings out and frowned at them. Finally a smile curled the back edges of her pointed beak.

"I did fly!" she cheeped. "I can fly!"

Flea sprang from the branch and flew to the apple tree. She went to the very top, then flew back to the pecan tree. Chirping and smiling, she swooped down and landed, light as a feather, on my back.

"Gray, did you see that? Did you see me? I can fly. *I CAN FLY!*"

She gave a little hop and took off again. It made me smile when she climbed and climbed, so high into the blue sky that I could hardly see her. Then she held her wings against her sides and dived. I held my breath. At the last second, just before it seemed as if she would smash into the ground, she spread her wings. She swooped back up into the sky again. She turned left. She turned right. She flew right through the middle of the pecan tree without touching a single branch or leaf.

"I can fly! I can fly! I can fly!"

And she did.

She flew from one tree to the next. She flew up. She flew down. She even flew at the woodpile a few times, chirping her threats at Bullsnake. Then she swooped to the porch and landed on my back. She gave me a sweet little peck on the cheek and thanked me for not eating her. She thanked me for feeding her grasshoppers. She thanked me for teaching her how to fly.

Then my little Flea flew away.

CHAPTER 11

A couple of weeks after Flea left, the Mama lct me spend the night inside the house. It was the first time I ever got to spend that long inside. It was kind of interesting. I wanted to explore and see what all the new smells were. Callie told me to curl up on the couch and pretend to be asleep—at least until the Mama and Daddy dozed off. Once they were in bed, she told me I could explore. But she warned me to be very quiet, or they would put me outside again.

The next morning Mama put Callie and me on the front porch. It was awfully cold. There was this strange white stuff all over the grass. Leaves on the pecan tree were all brown and lots of them had fallen to the ground. They were covered with the white stuff, too. Crisp and crunchy, they crackled beneath my paws.

I took a quick hunt, but didn't find a trophy to bring back to the mat. Callie was curled up in the rocking chair when I got to the porch. She yawned and looked at me.

"Why the long whiskers, Gray?"

I looked down—my whiskers were drooping. I twitched them a couple of times, but they still hung low.

"Your tail's been dragging the ground for the last couple of weeks, too."

Turning to the side, I looked back. Sure enough, my tail was hanging down, almost touching the porch. I flipped it once, then curled it around and sat on it.

"I don't know," I said. "I just don't feel too happy, I guess."

Callie hopped down from her rocker. She strolled right up to me and rubbed her cheek against mine.

"Feeling kind of sad and lonely?"

"Yeah. I guess that's it."

"Kind of miss that stupid bird, huh?"

I shrugged my ears. "Well . . . sort of. I can't help worrying about her. It's really cold. I wonder if she's all right. I wonder where she is. She might be stuck in some tree, shivering, with her little beak chattering. She might be sick or lost or—"

"Flea is just fine." Callie purred. "Birds know the way south. She had a good start before it turned cold. She will be okay."

I twitched my face again, but my whiskers still hung down.

"Then why do I feel so bad?"

Callie rubbed against my other cheek.

"You shouldn't feel bad. Flea would have never made it through the winter. Not here. She had to fly south. You *know* you did the right thing."

"I know. But . . . well . . . I didn't know it would hurt so bad. I thought when you do the right thing, you're supposed to feel good inside. I don't. I feel sad and lonely. I miss those little birdy claws scratching my back. I miss her yelling: 'Feed me!' I miss . . . I miss my Flea."

Callie leaned against my shoulder.

"Remember—I told you it wouldn't be easy?"

"I remember." I nodded. "But I thought you were talking about getting Bullsnake to help us. I thought that was what you meant when you said it wouldn't be easy."

"Well, yes, that too. But I also meant teaching Flea how to fly. Giving her enough faith in herself so that she could go south for the winter." Callie kissed me on the cheek and curled up beside me. "Sometimes doing the right thing hurts. But even when it hurts, it is still the right thing."

I pouted. "It shouldn't be like that."

"Maybe not," Callie agreed. "But that's the way it is. Besides, Flea will be back."

I raised my head. When I did, I saw my whiskers spring up.

"Are you sure?"

"Yes." Callie smiled. "Birds always come home in the spring."

"When is the spring?"

"It comes after winter—when the grass starts to grow again and when the trees get their buds. Grasshoppers will come back. June bugs will come back. Bird will come back and build a new nest in the apple tree. And . . ."

"And," I urged.

"And your little Flea will come back, too."

"Promise?"

"Promise."

I felt better already. My whiskers went up. When I walked toward the field for another mouse hunt, my tail was up, too. Then all at once I realized how close I was to the barn. Ever since the rats tried to get me, I'd made a wide arch around it. When I found myself right by the open doorway, my hair fuzzed to a sharp ridge down my back. My tail puffed.

I didn't run away from the barn, though, I just

walked really fast. At the edge of the field I paused and glanced back over my shoulder. Eyes tight, I glared at the open doorway. By spring I would be older. I would be bigger and stronger and braver. I could hardly wait until spring.

It was two days later when the House Mama finally let me in for the winter. It was worth the wait. I could eat cat food any time that I wanted it. In the evenings Mama opened a can of something that smelled delicious. Callie got to eat first, but she always left me plenty of the good stuff. There were even mice to chase and snack on. Mama really liked it when I got a house mouse. She would praise me and rub me while we sat on the couch.

Sometimes I would get in trouble when I stretched my muscles and raced through the house. It was even worse when I sharpened my claws on the couch. Mama would chase me with a rolled-up newspaper, and I had to hide for a while. I had lots of hiding places. I took long catnaps, and when I got up, Mama usually forgot all about the things that I did that she didn't like.

My favorite hiding place was in the window, behind the curtain. I could watch the winter birds eating seeds out of the feeder that Mama filled each morning. They didn't see me hiding

there. Sometimes I would reach out to them. I looked for Flea, but she didn't come to the feeder.

I felt stupid! I missed that silly bird. I wouldn't admit it to anyone but Callie, but I would like to have my friend back on my head.

I could hardly wait until spring.

ABOUT THE AUTHORS

CAROL WALLACE taught second grade for twenty-six years.

BILL WALLACE taught fourth grade and was an elementary school principal. Carol had an idea for a story about her gray cat, but she wasn't sure if she could write it or not. Bill has written twenty-three books for children and young adults.

High school sweethearts and married since 1966, they have joined forces for a number of projects—namely, raising three children and lots of pets. So, it seemed only natural to get together and write a story and two sequels about Gray.

"We had so much fun working together," they agreed, "we may try it again with another one of our animals."

Don't miss these books by

CAROL WALLACE AND BILL WALLACE

THE FLYING FLEA, CALLIE, AND ME

Callie was getting too old for the job, so the house people picked me to be a mouser. But I didn't plan on getting dive-bombed by a mockingbird building her nest...or adopting the baby who fell out. No joke! Flea—that's what I named her—couldn't even fly. She was pathetic. I had to help her. The first step was protecting Flea—and me—from the monster rats in the barn and Bullsnake under the woodpile. Next, Callie and I had to teach Flea to fly. After all, how could she stay up North with us when her bird family was flying to Florida. I know I'll miss my Flea. But she'll come back—after she's seen the world!

THAT FURBALL PUPPY AND ME
(Coming in Hardcover October 1999)

Here I am, a self-respecting kitten just trying to survive in a rat-eat-cat world, when the humans in my life start acting crazy. Something about the kids, and grandkids, coming to visit for Christmas. Mama accusing me of tearing up the presents. Noisy voices and grabby little hands. If the grandkids are bad, they're nothing compared to the gift the kids gave Mama for Christmas...a puppy! Dumb furball. Everybody is cooing over this yappy puppy who only wants to play. So I got him in trouble for tearingup the kitchen. Big deal. Problem is, I feel responsible. This puppy's headed for T*R*O*U*B*L*E. How can Isave him? I can't even save myself!

A MINSTREL® BOOK
Published by Pocket Books

Don't Miss These Fun Animal Adventures From

BILL WALLACE

UPCHUCK AND THE ROTTEN WILLY

Cats and dogs just can't be friend—or can they?

Iowa Children's Choice Award Master List 2000-2001
Indian Paintbrush Award Master List 1999-2000
Nevada Young Readers Award Master List 1999-2000

AND

UPCHUCK AND THE ROTTEN WILLY: THE GREAT ESCAPE

It's a dog's life—as told by a cat.

 A MINSTREL® BOOK

Available from Minstrel® Books
Published by Pocket Books

2300-01